S0-BEJ-000

ONCE UPON A TREE

ONCE UPON A TREE

DAWN JAROCKI
and SOREN KISIEL

ILLUSTRATED BY
JESSICA MCCLURE

PLUM BLOSSOM
BOOKS

Once upon a time,
        upon a tree,
    there was a leaf.

Every morning, the leaf stretched
toward the sun's first light.

Every evening, the leaf bathed in the amber glow of the sunset.

The leaf loved the morning rays, the evening rays, and all the rays in between.

One spring day, the leaf woke up to the sound of chattering birds.

"What's happening?" called the leaf.

A bird spread his wings wide. "I'm learning to fly!" he said.

"Fly?" asked the leaf. It had never thought
of that. "How do you learn to fly?"

The bird cocked his head sideways.

"I feel it inside," he said.

The leaf searched inside for the urge to fly.

There was nothing there.

"Should I fly, too?" the leaf asked.

"I don't know!" said the bird. "You're a leaf.
You need to figure out what leaves do."

Then he leaped off the branch and soared into the air.

"Wait!" the leaf called. "How am I supposed to know what leaves do?"

But by now the bird was far away, tumbling on the wind.

For days, the leaf worried over this question. It hardly noticed the morning's warm rays.

At night, the leaf shook in the wind.

Then, one evening, the leaf saw a plump caterpillar crawling along a branch. The caterpillar

     stopped,

          dangled,

and began gently wrapping herself in soft white silk.

"What are you doing?" asked the leaf.

"Hmmm?" mumbled the caterpillar. "I'm making a cocoon."

"Why?" asked the leaf.

The caterpillar thought for a moment.

"I don't know," she said. "I just feel like doing it."

The leaf searched inside for the urge to make a cocoon.

There was nothing there.

"Should I make a cocoon too?" the leaf asked.

"Don't ask me," said the caterpillar. "You're a leaf. You need to figure out what leaves do."

"How am I supposed to know?" cried the leaf.

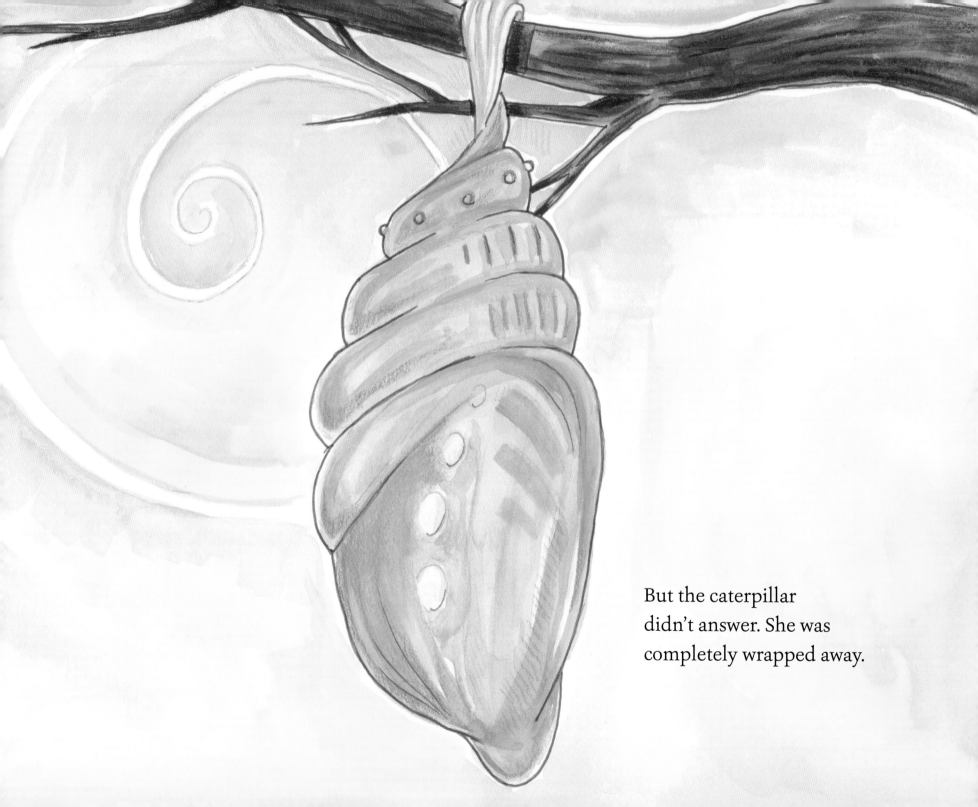

But the caterpillar
didn't answer. She was
completely wrapped away.

For weeks the leaf sat, staring at the cocoon.

Each day, the sun rose and warmed the air.

But the leaf no longer paid any attention.

Finally, the cocoon
twitched,
turned,
and split open.

Out came damp, glistening wings.

The caterpillar, now a butterfly, stretched her wings
out like the rays of the sun.

The leaf could hardly bear to look. They were so beautiful.

"I knew that was a good idea," the butterfly said.

"How did you know?" the leaf asked.

But the butterfly had already flown away,   zigzagging through the air.

Sometimes the top of a tree can be a lonely place.

The leaf worried.

The days grew shorter. The breezes blew harder. But the leaf no longer noticed anything but the thoughts spinning in its head.

It held tightly to the tree in the chilly winds,
    wrapped in its worries,
                exhausted.

"Hi, leaf!" came a voice. "Aren't you a beautiful shade of red?" The bird that had learned to fly so many months ago landed in a flurry of shining feathers.

The leaf looked at itself. It was true, the leaf had turned a beautiful crimson color. But it hadn't paid a moment's notice.

"Bird!" the leaf called out. "Tell me again about that feeling you had inside when it was time to learn to fly."

The bird cocked his head.

"I don't remember," he said.

"How can you not remember?" the leaf shouted.

"Are you angry at me?" the bird asked.

"Yes!"

The leaf filled up with fury
at the bird,
at the butterfly,
and at a world where everything but the
leaf seemed to know what it wanted.

"Well," said the bird, "right now I have the feeling that it would be nice to fly off that way." He nodded his beak in a southerly direction. "Do you feel that too?"

"I don't know!" cried the leaf. "*Should* I feel that?"

The bird looked sideways at the leaf.

"I don't feel like I *should* feel like flying that way. I just *feel* like flying that way. It's getting cold around here, don't you think?"

For the first time in many weeks the leaf noticed the air.

"I feel cold!" said the leaf.

"What else do you feel?" asked the bird.

The leaf sat still.

It noticed the sunbeams piercing the clouds. It noticed its branch swaying in the wind. And it stretched into the golden light.

"I feel," said the leaf slowly, "like this tree is my home."

"That sounds nice," said the bird.

The leaf felt the brilliant sunshine warming it, even through the cold air.

"I feel like this tree *is* me," said the leaf.

"I think that the sunlight and the air and
  I have a job to do
      right here
    together."

"Wow!" said the bird. He ruffled his feathers with joy for the leaf.

"And I feel," whispered the leaf to itself, "like I could just–"

The leaf started to relax its tight grip on the branch…

But no! It had just figured out that this branch was right where it belonged.

The leaf looked inside itself again. There it was—clear as the blue sky.

"Bird," the leaf said, "I think it might be time to fly after all."

And with that, in the glow of
the evening sunset, the leaf

just

let

go.

A breeze caught
the leaf and carried
it away from the
branch.

It caught glimpses of the
tree—its tree—against the
deep blue sky.

The leaf stretched into
the breeze.

It swirled
and it twirled
and it danced
in the amber
light.

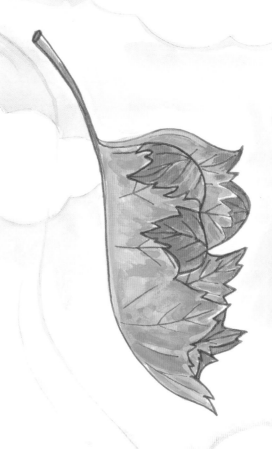

The bird looked down at the leaf from the branch high above.

"Well then," he said, "I guess that's what you ought to do."

And with that, the bird leaped from the branch, and went where his wings took him.

RELATED TITLES FROM PARALLAX PRESS

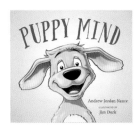

For Elijah, my ray of sunshine. —D.J.

For Katie, always my inspiration to learn to fly. —S.K.

Text © 2017 Dawn Jarocki
and Soren Kisiel

Illustrations
© 2017 Jessica McClure

Cover and interior design
by Debbie Berne

ISBN: 978-1-941529-74-4

All Rights Reserved
Printed in Korea

No part of this book may
be reproduced in any form
or by any means, electronic
or mechanical, without
permission in writing from
the publisher.

Library of Congress
Cataloging-in-Publication
Data is available upon
request.

Plum Blossom Books,
the children's imprint of
Parallax Press, publishes
books on mindfulness
for young people and the
grown-ups in their lives.

Parallax Press
P.O. Box 7355
Berkeley, CA 94707
parallax.org

1 2 3 4 5 / 21 20 19 18 17